# A Moon Among Stars

*by Jessica and Dave Dever*

LANIER PRESS

**LANIER PRESS**

Alpharetta, GA

ISBN: 978-1-61005-815-5
Library of Congress Control Number: 2016948562

10 9 8 7 6 5 4 3 2     0 5 2 6 1 6

Printed in the United States of America

∞ This paper meets the requirements of ANSI/NISO Z39.48-1992 (Permanence of Paper)

Background photography by Tony DeCaires and David Dever II

Our story begins
just like a normal day.
The sun came up
and the moon went away.

Moon, go away.
Moon?

"No!" humphed Moon.
"I will not rest.

It's not fair
that Sun is favored best.

Sun brings happiness and
makes days bright.

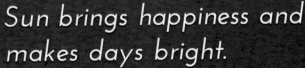

I'm not happy or sad,
just a reflected light."

"When Sun is out, the people play. When I am out, they all go away."

"Sun's rays of light
help the trees to grow,
cause flowers to bloom,
and melt away snow."

"I just tell people it's time for bed.
I don't help anything grow, or have joy to spread.

It's always so dark, with lightbulbs as light.
I want to see day; I don't want to bring night."

"So I have decided
that I'm calling it quits.

I'm through with the night.
This job is the pits!"

"Hey there, Moon," said Cloud.
"Why the big frown?

If there wasn't a moon,
        this world would come unwound."

"So people may not play outside in the night.

Some animals are nocturnal and wake up to your light."

Firefly

Raccoon

Bat

Owl

Hedgehog

Red-eyed tree frog

"Your job is important—
much more than you know.

You help in the Earth's rotation
and decide when tides flow."

## MOON PHASES

WAXING

FIRST QUARTER

CRESCENT

GIBBOUS

NEW MOON

FULL MOON

GIBBOUS

LAST QUARTER

CRESCENT

WANING

"You have so many phases
that illuminate the night,
from your waning crescent to
your full moon so bright."

MOON LANDING

"People live their whole lives studying just you,
hoping to one day walk on the moon."

Cloud winked at Moon.
He did all he could do.

He drifted away, saying . . .
    "Moon, just be you."

Moon rose with pride
the very next night,

happy to wake up
his friends with his light.

He smiled alongside
the stars in the sky,

and cherished the
rise and fall of the lunar tide.

He never again
    wanted to be someone new.

Hey, listen up now,
    because the same goes for you . . .

You are unique,
so be who you are.
You just may find yourself
a moon among stars.

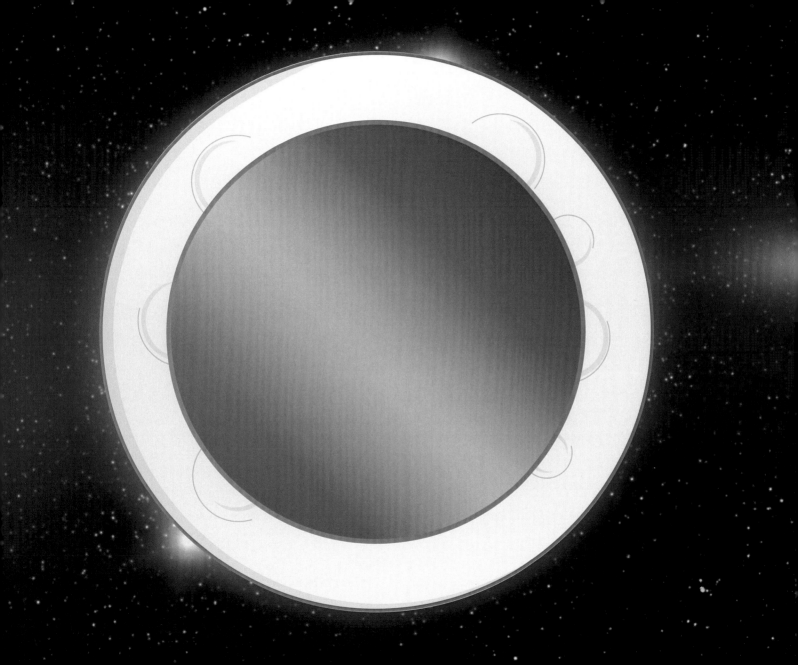

The creative husband-and-wife team behind *A Moon Among Stars* is anything but normal. They've both been bitten by the creative bug that keeps them continually thinking and expressing themselves in various ways. Dave is co-owner of Revel Pix, a multipurpose creative production house that provides complete video and motion solutions to his clients. Jessica is a pre-K teacher. She is state-certified and recently earned her graduate degree in math, science, and technology education from St. John Fisher College.

This is the first of hopefully many books by the Devers. They reside in Rochester, New York, love the Buffalo Bills, and take very serious photos in front of fences.